FLAP YOUR WINGS

A Random House PICTUREBACK®

P. D. Eastman

Flap Your

The Library of Congress has cataloged this work as follows: Eastman, Philip D. Flap your wings/P.D. Eastman.—New York: Random House, c1977. [32] p.: col. ill.; 21 cm.—(A Random House pictureback) (The Best book club ever) SUMMARY: When Mr. and Mrs. Bird discover a strange egg in their nest they try to hatch it. ISBN: 0-394-83565-4 [1. Birds—Fiction. 2. Alligators—Fiction] I. Title. PZ7.E1314 F1 1977 [E] 76-24164 MARC Library of Congress 78 AC ISBN: 0-394-83443-7 (B.C.); 0-394-83565-4 (trade); 0-394-90839-2 (lib. bdg.)
Manufactured in the United States of America 1 2 3 4 5 6 7 8 9 0

Wings

Random House New York

A boy came down the path.
An egg lay in the path.
The boy saw the egg.

"Someone might step on that egg
and break it," he said. He looked around.

He saw flamingos and frogs, and turtles and alligators.
"Whose egg is this?" he called. But nobody answered.

Then the boy looked up. He saw an empty nest in a tree.
"Here is an egg without a nest," he said, "and there is a nest
without an egg."

The boy climbed
the tree.

He put the egg in the nest.
Then he went away.

Mr. and Mrs. Bird came home. They were surprised
to find an egg in their nest.
"That's not *our* egg," said Mrs. Bird. "Look how big it is!"

"But it is an egg. It's in our nest," said Mr. Bird.
"If an egg is in your nest, you sit on it and keep it warm.
It doesn't matter whose egg it is."

"All right," said Mrs. Bird. "But I wonder what kind
of bird is going to come out of that egg."

They took turns keeping the egg warm.

First Mrs. Bird
sat on it.

Then Mr. Bird
sat on it.

And sometimes, because it was so big, they both sat on it. "I still wonder what kind of bird is going to come out of this egg," said Mrs. Bird.

One day Mrs. Bird heard a squeaking noise.
"Help!" she said. "This egg is squeaking!"

Mr. Bird came back to the nest. He listened to the egg.

"The egg is not squeaking," Mr. Bird said. "It's our baby that is squeaking. He is ready to come out of the egg."

Mr. and Mrs. Bird waited. What kind of bird was going to come out of their egg?

The egg started to crack.

Then it cracked some more.

And there was the baby!

Mr. Bird was very excited.
"It's Junior!" he shouted. "What a beautiful baby!"

Junior opened his mouth. It was a big mouth and it was full of teeth.

"That's the funniest looking baby I ever saw," said Mrs. Bird. "Something is wrong. I don't think he's our baby at all!"

"He's in our nest, so he must be ours," said Mr. Bird. "His mouth is open. That means he's hungry. When your baby is hungry, you feed him."

"All right," said Mrs. Bird. "But I wonder what he's going to look like when he grows up."

Mr. and Mrs. Bird went away to get some food for Junior.

Mr. Bird brought
a pink worm.

Mrs. Bird brought
a green one.

Junior swallowed
both worms in one gulp.
Then he opened his mouth
wide again.

"We have to get Junior
lots more to eat,"
said Mr. and Mrs. Bird.

Hour after hour, day after day, they got food for Junior.

Mrs. Bird got berries and cherries,

butterflies and caterpillars,

dragonflies and mosquitoes,

ladybugs and tiger beetles.

Mr. Bird got crickets
and spiders,

grasshoppers
and snails,

red ants and
black ants,

and centipedes, too!

"What kind of bird eats so much?"
said Mrs. Bird.

"It doesn't matter," said Mr. Bird.
"He's still hungry and we have to feed him."
    Weeks went by. Junior never stopped eating.
And he never stopped being hungry.

But also . . .

...he never
stopped growing.

He grew **bigger**...

and **bigger**...

and **bigger!**

Finally Junior got so big that Mr. Bird said,
"It's getting too crowded up here. Junior has to
leave the nest. It is time for him to fly away."

"You are right," said Mrs. Bird.
"The time has come. Junior has to be pushed
out of the nest. We must show him how to fly."

Mrs. Bird pushed and pushed.
While Mrs. Bird pushed,

Mr. Bird showed Junior how to fly.
  "Jump into the air like this," he said.
"Then flap your wings."

Junior got ready. He took a big
breath and jumped into the air.
Up…up…up went Junior.

"Flap your wings!"
yelled Mrs. Bird.

"Flap your wings!"
yelled Mr. Bird.

Junior flapped and flapped. He flapped everything he had.
But it didn't do any good because he didn't have any wings.
Down...down...down went Junior.

Down he went with a big SPLASH into the water.

It was wet in the water. It was cool and
comfortable. It was just right for Junior.

Mrs. Bird looked down from the tree.

"You know," she said to Mr. Bird, "I don't think Junior was a bird at all!"

"It doesn't matter," Mr. Bird said.

"He's happy now. And just look at him swim!"